KUTTI DETECTIVE: HOW IT BEGAN

DETECTIVE FICTION

AYHAM BICHA

Made with ♥ on the Notion Press Platform
www.notionpress.com

THIS BOOK IS DEDICATED TO

YOU

Contents

Foreword

This book is yet another amazing work of my son, Ayham. He has taken much efforts in writing this book and I am really impressed and happy that he has reached so far. My wishes, prayers and support will always be with him.

He has always been fond of detective novels and stories but I never thought that one day he would be an author of one too!

You have always made me proud and I hope I was able to support you even in the most difficult times.

Preface

Hello there!

My name is **Ayham Bicha**, a student, currently pursuing my +2 studies in commerce stream. Am an emerging anchor, a passionate public speaker, content creator, author, storyteller as well as a trainer.

Some of my major achievements include: I was the recipient of ORMA Orator of the Year Award 2023, National Champion of Public speaking 2021, finalist of World Gavelier Championship 2022, I've been honoured with the National Outstanding Scout for the year 2021-22(Bharat Scout and Guides), India Book of Record holder for 'Youngest Trainer', Table Topic Champion 2022, Extempore Champion in the district level comptition of CBSE Kalotsav, Keynote speaker of PMI Asia Regional Conference 2022 along with Dr.Kiran Bedi (Former Lieutanant Governer of Puduchery) and have recieved several other accolades in school, district and state levels.

My hobbies are reading, gardening, making videos and playing football.

The Kutti Detective books marks my entry to the world of literature where I write out of my imagination as an aspiring detective.

Acknowledgements

First and foremost, let me acknowlededge my dear mother for her love, care, guidance and motivation. Without her, all my feats would not be possible. She is and will be my greatest rolemodel and superhero of my life.

Next, I would like to acknowledge my friend and classmate, Fidha, for her contribution to this book as an illustrator. Thank you for taking your time and drawing these beautiful pictures.

To all my well-wishers, friends and teachers, thank you so much for your support and encouragement.

Last but not the least, let me thank the Almighty for guiding me through the right path and for all his blessings.

Prologue

This book is just a mere imagination of a 17-year old boy, who is making his dream a reality through the fictitious character 'Kutti Detective'.

A culmination of my childhood acts as a detective officer, police officer and an army officer have been carefully illustrated and assigned to each and every character. This book travels through the journey of 'Kutti Detective' becoming well, a detective! Sharing some sweet and painful memories of his childhood days and taking along through his life filled with mysteries, setbacks, thrills and wits.

The story is narrated in a childish way along with some maturity in certain aspects to inform everyone to be who we are.

"All characters mentioned are truly fictitious."

KUTTI DETECTIVE

HOW IT BEGAN

CHAPTER ONE

A TRUTH CAN'T BE HIDDEN FOR LONG

Before I get to anything, I gotta say, being a detective of yourself is something else, it's tough to crack the mysteries hidden inside us. Yes, today was one such day!

When did I become so conscious about myself? Is it due to the age or is it just me being lost in the excitement of tomorrow's event? Sorry for the rough start, there's simply a lot going on in my mind, and I don't know how to begin.

It was a hassle of a day! We were on the search of getting a, not a clue, but a stupid dress. I'm not even kidding; I'd have literally been able to solve 2 cases in the time of finding a good suit for me. Something, which looks elegant, formal, and classy. I hope you could relate. You might have found a costume which you liked, but the size won't be available, sometimes it would be the price, sometimes it would be the design of this and that or something else.......at least the girls can relate to this, right? No joke, you really have got the potential to become a phenomenal detective.

Yes, at last, after examining almost each and every store, my mum bought a nice tuxedo for me, literally from the shop we entered to first. I was happy though. We billed and got back to home, to find out my biggest problem, the event is tomorrow and I've not prepared ANYTHING!! I grabbed some papers, started scribbling something.... then after a while, crumbled it and threw it to the bin, I took the next paper and the same thing happened. I didn't know what to do! I reached out my hands to my wafer roll packet.... (which contains my cigars of course), only to find there is none left! I finished the entire packet and time was going as fast as it could. I was completely puzzled. But luckily, every mystery has an answer. I took my K.D and went through it, checking whether I could get some inspiration from it. Even though, I've dealt with many cases, there was just a few accounts in the K.D. The most prominent one being CASE NO#11, where I heroically solved the mystery of Ivory Turn and got the revenge-blooded Rachel Livingston into custody. And hence, I found the answer to the question: what should I do or speak? Thus, leaving me to write this book.......

Ugh! I hate to do this but I guess at one point or the other, the world has to know this secret. The grand mystery of how did I become a Kutti Detective. It's funny, isn't? Who would have thought a detective who's an expert at cracking mysteries, has a mystery himself! I'm afraid to continue, but it seems that I'm out of options.

Well, people say that there is a mystery in everything or everyone, and once it gets revealed, you understand 'em in a much better way. In my case, it's pretty weird. I'm no certainly an ordinary detective! Who else can solve about 15 cases at this young age! Am I being too proud, sorry if I was! I too have got a few friends who boasts around mainly about their family and their businesses and here's me, a guy who's killed his own parents! You read it correctly. I'm a murderer who's apparently skilled in finding murderers too.

Is it confusing? So, was my life. How else could a person, no, more precisely, a child's life be if he was isolated for 7 years! I'm not what you see me outside! I've a completely different story, which I'm not proud of, of course. But it pains me to reveal it......I always wished that no one.......... ugh! I don't know!.........The truth can't be hidden for long....

CHAPTER TWO

MY VILLAGE LIFE

It was in the year of 1956, on November 1st, at 2:00AM, the cries of a joyful new born baby brought happiness in the poorly lighted Government medical hospital. It was a historical birth; a baby boy and a state (Kerala) being formed on the same day. I was born as the heir to a Panchayat President and a housewife. So lovely was my birth, that I became famous at an instant. What else could you expect if your village is surrounded by gossiper's...

"The kid who escaped from death", "The kid who killed his mother", "The Panchayath President has an autistic son", the kid that.... the kid this.... what all could be said, and spread.... they did. There were even some who believed that I was a God and that's why Kerala is known as God's Own Country!

I'm sure that they could write a 500-page novel in less than a day, each chapter describing a person. But don't worry, none of that nonsense was true!

Anyhow, I was born and bought up in the scenic village of Maranjarikkad, a place surrounded by forests. If you were to visit, you should come early in the morning to enjoy that marvellous sunrise and take a quick refreshing bath in the cold waters of 'Vishalaya', the stream which

I was born as the heir to a Panchayat President and a housewife.

flows through our village. My father had no time for me nor for my mom.... he was a people's man. He was quite stern of a guy, political in his views, had a perfectly trimmed thick moustache, wore the classic half-sleeved white shirt and white lungi with a wine-red border line. His face had some curls and scars here and there, his voice was fascinating with a great bass to it and one thing which was appealing about him was his dyed, oiled hair, very neatly combed. He adored his hair and moustache more than anything else and only allowed Kochuppa, the barber to touch it. He'd leave the home early in the morning, go to the tea shop, then roam about in the village, stop for lunch at home, then again goes for rounds and would come back home drunk, that was his routine....

Now, my mum's case was different, she was so sweet and caring. She played with me, told me stories, gave me food and put me to sleep. She was also of the bold type and possessed a serious face. You can never tell that my mom and father are couples, rather, they look like siblings. My mom young, and my father in his 40's, both having a similar face cut. But unfortunately, when I grew up, my father used to take me with him, and thus we got separated. But she didn't argue at all, she would look after me in the night and that would be the only time, she wears a happy face.... I still wonder how she spent her time in our hut all alone. Loneliness is unbearable, at least for me, especially with what I have experienced. But if I'm in the middle of a case, I'd like to be as alone as possible, running away from all tensions, focusing, communicating to my mind, reframing the happenings.

My father has this only negative of coming home drunk, otherwise he is an honest, sincere man. All the natives liked him and he would be the first person to approach if there was any help. It was when he started taking me round the village, I started studying a lot about him. I, myself, was proud to be the son of such a respectable man. You see, from my birth onwards I was a keen observer. I, even now, know every tip and turn of Maranjarikkad. Trust me, when you step out of your cribs, you will automatically understand that there is more to explore in this world that is so vast and beautiful. Life was all well, until, the tragedy happened. No man likes another of his species to be successful. I'm not saying everyone is like this, but there are some, overcome by selfishness, jealousy, and all of those destructive emotions. As I've said my father was an honest and respectable man, who fought against injustice and worked for the welfare of his people. Our village was rich in rubber, so there were many interest groups who liked to establish a factory. I'm not elaborating but I hope you, yourself can make a narrative of what all could have happened. (you should know by now that I'm not a fan of writing). To them, there was just one hindrance and that was my poor father. Our hut became a regular place of bullying.... We, no, literally the entire village were tortured.

At last, Maranjarikkad found its ill-fate. The guardian and the president, more importantly my father was killed and that too, right in front of my face.......

CHAPTER THREE

THE TURNING POINT

An unforgettable murder at the alley. Excuse me for a minute... Let me get my thoughts together... It was due to this reason; I was afraid to share it to you.

Seeing my own father get shot.... I was traumatised, my mum was no longer serious, she wept all day. Our hut had this strange atmosphere which I'm not able to explain. The FIR was filed, investigations went down. Maranjarikkad went silent, not even a bird could be heard chirruping, the leaves were still, even the sound of the small waves of Vishalaya were diminishing, everything seemed quiet.

The case was taken to the court, and the worst drawback of democracy was unveiled.... power, money, position, influence all merged in, making.... the son of the president the killer! Me.

My mom fainted, the courtroom saw a revolt, but justice had been made, I was sentenced for imprisonment for 7 years! With my innocent thoughts, I couldn't get a flavour of what was happening, all I knew was that I'm going to be shut somewhere, separated from a village which was kept close to my heart and my mom who was there in each and every breath of mine. That poor woman seeing my puzzled nature, hugged me, started crying her eyes out and convinced me that I was going to a school and you will be learning many things and would come out as a great person.

As innocent as I could ever be, I asked her, "But why mamma?"

She couldn't help herself, she wiped her tears, kissed me on my forehead and said, "Don't worry, you trust me don't you sweetheart? I'll be waiting for you outside...ok?" saying this she kissed me once again and I was taken away by the police and all I could remember was that the next day, I had woken up in a completely new room. It had a strange scent and not even a lantern hung inside.

I still used to think, where did this aspect of humanity go that day at the courtroom, what about mercy!? How could you think so ruthlessly? What even is Democracy?

I was desperate those days. All alone and no one to talk. Didn't I tell you that loneliness was unbearable, it was solely due to this part of my life. The silence and moments of isolation always tempted me to think of my beautiful and happy days with my mother, how I used to run about, making problems for my chitty-chatty neighbour, Ausamma, or the days when Rajuettan gave me that cup of hot milk coupled with a crispy banana fry, my outings, though short but certainly sweet, with my father and suddenly the worst picture would pop up. My father lying dead in the streets beside a streetlight. My helplessness nature.... I had no idea of the place which I was enclosed in or of what was happening until to my relief, I found out a companion who surprisingly appeared to be my uncle, Krishna Kumar! He was the only officer whom I saw a smile upon. He was formidable but of the jolly type and it was then I really started to believe that this was a school. He taught me many things, the alphabets, the numbers, I guess he was bored too, roaming, patrolling, so he spent most of his time with me.

But he never gave me answers to my questions of where am I? Which is this place? When can I meet my mom? And a lot other's.... Then, I stopped asking.

As I grew up, K.K, that was what I called him, allowed me to accompany in his walks and my observant behaviour led me to study this place in less than a week. I became more familiar to this place. I knew a lot about it, much more than the senior most officers who have worked here.

One day, K.K realised my skill to observe, recall and reframe everything. It was when they were in a conversation about a prisoner's escape, I interfered and narrated what could have happened. At the end, I was right after all!

"There is this portion at the far end corner which is covered with bushes. Whoever was the man, he had been prepping his escape. You see once you remove the metal the soil is very moist and can be easily dug out. As it is an isolated corner, no one would really bother, so it could be executed easily. Moreover, the hole dug out will not be visible due to the bushes. Once dug, considerably deep you can enter the pipeline hole which is under construction based on the project of the Indian Government. Then, while navigating inside that tunnel, with someone's assistance, he or she can escape and reach the construction site. Then, a person must have picked him up and hallelujah, he's escaped!"

As I finished my conclusions, I saw the jaw-dropped faces of K.K and the other officer.

"But how in earth, do you know all of these!?" asked K.K in wonder!

I walked off proudly, quite amazed with myself.

"Well, many mysteries can unravel before you if you just open your eyes wide and pay keen attention to your surroundings. If you need any other help, I'll be at my cell." I walked off proudly, quite amazed with myself.

CHAPTER FOUR

BEHIND THE ESCAPER

After a while, just as expected, K.K entered my cell and with great hesitation, he spoke "Uh, Kichu.... (enters my cell) .... you seem to know a lot about this place.... It would be great if you could, well, help us find out that person.... He is a wanted criminal and if we can't find him before others find it out, it would be a great problem.... I hope you understand."

"Well, there isn't much use to run after him. But.... (I stopped for a minute as a great idea struck me) ... anyways, I'll help you out. Let's do this step by step, first: go through the list of those who visited him and then get the whereabouts of the last visitor. If my assumptions are to be right, that person would have visited John, uhm.... (I coughed and there was an awkward silence) Oh, God, K.K, that poem of "Jhonny, Jhonny, yes papa" has really taken on my mind. Alright, where was I? Yes, yes, so that last visitor must have visited him on the day he escaped, track him, interrogate him, whatever and you will have the answer! That's it, all the best!"

When the officer's left my cell, I called out to K.K and said, "One more thing K.K, (in a low tone), if my intuitions are right, then he, most probably, would be dead."

"But how can you say so precisely?" K.K looked at me with suspicion.

"I don't know, my mind says so. I feel like he has been shot down. Anyway, that isn't the point. If he is dead, all you've got to say is that he died during an encounter with you, you follow that, trust me K.K, please"

The officers hesitated to do what I said. I mean who would take orders from a kid. But due to the pressure, they followed my instructions and set out. The last visitor of the escaper (that's how we are going to call him) was a person named 'Michael'. After approximately 3 hours, they returned back, came to my cell and appreciated my wits.

"Thank you so much, Kichu, I see a great detective in you!" said the General of the Prison.

"Thank you so much sir, I'm really obliged with your kind words, so, I guess you found him."

K.K intervened and said that he unfortunately died as they had to shoot him down while he was running.

"Oh, that's sad to know. Anyhow, if any problems like these occur, be comfortable in approaching me"

As all the officers left one-by-one, K.K stood there and looked at me dead in the eye! "Yes.... Go ahead!" Said he in a firm voice.

"You good, K.K. What do you mean? You look a bit off the colour."

"Don't beat around the bush, Kichu. You killed him, didn't you? I appreciate your wits but no man can exactly tell that he or she would be dead. I did you a favour by saying exactly what you wished, now it's high time you return the favour...."

"Well, that's fair enough. Yes... your suspicions are indeed... right. It was ME who killed him."

15

CHAPTER FIVE

THE BEGINNING OF KUTTI DETECTIVE

"Whaaaaat!! why.... (K.K began to stagger) How could you? You playing games here or what!?"

"Oh, you say I am playing games. What about all the games which you have played. I'm not a kid anymore K.K! I'm 8 years old, eight! I've asked you a thousand times of why I'm here and about my mom, to which you didn't utter a word, not even a single word! I know K.K, almost everything. I'm locked in this place because I'm accused of killing my own father. How inhumane could that ever be? I've spent months trying to overcome that trauma. When I close my eyes, I'm immediately drifted to those days... When I accompany you in your patrolling, my thoughts are entirely of my dear father. And you thought that I would not recognise the escaper! The real killer of my father! His face is still there, deep down inside me. I'll never forget that brute's face. Never ever!"

"I'm, I am sorry, Kichu. I didn't mean to do it. But how did you kill him, when you are locked up here."

"I do understand and I'm sorry for my rough behaviour. You know, I'm not being able to recover from it. And killing the escaper, Mr. John, well... that was quite easy. I did exactly what I instructed you earlier. I kept a close eye on him and figured out what he was doing. I could easily make out when he would escape and I expected a visitor. That was one of the parts where I struggled. I had to be as childish as possible with the constable and saw the details he recorded, that was how I got the name of the visitor plus the escaper. Then, while I was there with you, I stole your rifle... Which, no offense, was quite easy."

"No wonder, I was missing a few bullets. But he didn't die in the tunnel, he was there in the streets. So...."

"Yeah, I escaped along with him, followed him all around and when the best moment came, (and the moment was that he realised someone was following him), I revealed my identity and shot him down like a true hero! Tuff! Haha."

"That isn't a story to be proud of, Kichu!"

"So, are you suggesting that the false story of me killing my own father is better?"

"I don't want to argue, but you have amazed me. You... you are a 'Kutti Detective', heh? How you extended your service to us, I appreciate. But what you did behind the curtain... Don't do that again. No wonder you always asked me to read that 'Sherlock Holmes' book, heh?"

"(grin) By the way, Kutti Detective... that's actually a good name and you know what, from today onwards I'm going to be known as that... The Great Kutti Detective!"

"That's a stretch! Ok, then... bye Kutti Detective and one more thing, don't take anything from me without my

I shot him down, like a true hero!

permission, right? Last warning!"

"I'll try not to... You know, there are a few more persons to catch..."

K.K looked at me gravely and left my cell.

CHAPTER SIX

JJ BROTHERS

It was a fine afternoon. The banyan tree protecting me from the scorching sunlight. In my childhood days, the waters of Vishalaya were my biggest companion, and as I'm locked up here, the banyan tree was where I spend my time.

We were taking rest after having our lunch. Today, it was special, we had chicken biriyani! You might be wondering, what's there to be excited about? You won't understand. Try this: for an entire week have bland dishes, the same one for every course, and then have a plate of chicken biriyani. That smell will lift you into heavens, just imagine that. Don't forget to have a glass of water or else you would end up choking.

But what was special? Our General got posting to another jail, so it was his treat and an expression of gratitude to all of us! Though we, I mean, they... are criminals, we all possess a kind heart, at least the inmates in **this** prison.

As we were sitting, playing games with our fellow inmates, K.K waved to me. He had a photo and a file in his hands. He looked tensed in his behaviour, hesitant in his actions and angry in his expressions. Ya, I have no idea how all of these are portrayed in one person itself. We walked to

The banyan tree was where I spend my time.

my cell and K.K started speaking,

"Here you go, Kichu." Saying this he passed over the file and the photo. As I set my eyes on the picture, I instantaneously realised who it was! The JJ brothers. Well, they aren't JJ now, I shot one of the J, Mr. John. This was his brother and business partner, Mr. Jovial, that was the name in the file.

"I know this person K.K. Though it was dark that day, the moonlight was enough for me to understand him. He is also an advocate, isn't he? I remember him being the prosecutor."

"Yes, you are perfectly right. He was the one who took up the case and made you the culprit in the eyes of everyone. So, I thought we could do a bit of business here."

"Woah K.K! That's surprising. What makes you do it? I remember someone

saying (in K.K's voice) 'Don't do that again, Kichu'."

K.K didn't like that impression of mine. His left eyebrow twitched and he gave me a look of displeasure. I apologised and he continued...

"Jovial has an eye on you. He believes that it was you who killed his brother but he can't really make that out due to your amazing execution."

I interrupted, "K.K, it's not 'he believes', he witnessed me killing him, just as he witnessed my father being shot."

"No way! You didn't say all this to me. No wonder! He is already taking steps to avenge that. He has threatened your mother, but don't worry, I moved her to the city. So, she would be quite all right. You better think of a plan, otherwise things are going to get out of hand."

"Hmm, ok. But why should I think of a plan, you seem to already have one."

"Yes, I do and we are going to do this in your Kutti Detective style. It's not just you who hates him, we all do... so, you up for it?"

"Just state your plan, K.K...." I said sharply.

"So, here's what we are going to do. We can take you out on remand, saying that you are going to help us with catching this wanted man. I can easily get the papers. Then, all we need to do is to catch him red-handed, we put him to jail and well, finish him, for our safety."

"Hmm, not bad. Honestly, I thought you would mess that up. But a few adjustments into it... Getting me out on remand... I don't think it'd be easy. You have got to convince the new general, who knows nothing of me. Then, finishing him in the prison, that can't happen. He has a lot of influence and power, so even if we arrest him, I don't think we can put him behind the bars. So, we have to play the same game as we did in John's case. Jovial died in an encounter, as simple as that. So, covering it up is also going to be easy. Then, no pressure, only safe execution."

"Hmm.... That sounds good. So, how we proceeding?"

"First, we need a strong case against him, so get that ready. Then, we, I mean, you have to work upon convincing whosoever is the new General... And we will make the steps after that. Most importantly, we have to inform the media, that the 'Kutti Detective' is going to investigate or help the police..."

"I don't think that's necessary... Informing the media, things will get complicated, moreover he will know that we are after him."

"Yes, that's what I need. It would make things thrilling, won't it? Otherwise for the readers, it would just be a tale of heroism and valour. We need some action from the villain! That would spice things up!"

"(in a sarcastic voice) As you wish sir! So, let me get the things ready. In the meantime, you think about what we can do after we get ou... Yes..."

A constable interrupted our talk and instructed K.K that the General wants to meet him.

As K.K left, I was shifted into a dreamworld. My thoughts were entirely of what all I could do when I'm out of this place which has evolved to be more like my home than a school. I thought of my dear mother, how did she spend her time, her serious face appeared onto my mind and I laughed, remembering those times when I used to trouble my mom. Ah, it was lovely. I wondered how she would be now. Perhaps, she has become an old lady. I thought about my father, how he would have been if he was alive. And I grinned again, that thick moustache becoming grey, wrinkles taking over his face, everything appeared so humorous! My thoughts, my imagination was suddenly interrupted as I heard sprinting footsteps coming to my cell. I sprang up from where I was laying down. It was none other than K.K, looking really tensed, his hands shivering, and his face showing horror and fear! That was my nature, the first thing which I do before anyone approaches me is study these three elements: Behaviour, Action, Expression. With that, I have understood the man and I would also know how to befriend him! But analysing those three elements ain't easy. Everyone has their own way of depicting their gestures and emotions. So, it would take time. In my case, it's an exception. My extraordinary observant skills help me to analyse a person in no time! Kutti Detective things, you know. Oh, no! Where was I? Yeah, if I start praising myself, then I always lose my track.

K.K came to me and said, "Kichu, things have gone out of hand. Jo...Jov...Jovial he, he is coming here!"

"What!" I was amazed and couldn't speak anything else.

"Well, here's the action you wanted! The new general is his guy. Jovial is going to come tomorrow and to YOUR cell."

"Alright, that's not good... That ruins our entire plan. So, one will walk out, heh? No problems, we will see how we are going to do... Don't panic, K.K. We have got this..." Though I was confident, calm and composed in my words, my inside was burning... with literal fear and terror!

"All I got to say is... All the Best." And K.K ran back in the same speed to where he came from.

CHAPTER SEVEN

JOVIAL ENTERS

I, honestly, was terrified with the thought of that gigantic man coming here. I had zero idea on what to do. I was awake, the entire night, deeply thinking. I am, no joke, an ant to him. But I strongly believed that my story was not going to end soon. An evil man might win once or twice but one day, one day he is going to face his fate in the most painful way, he is going to be brought to the limelight. Jovial is not just evil, he is hell in the lives of many. He has great influence over everyone, and a lot of money. To him, money is paper. He simply throws it around. I at times, used to think, what joy does he get from it? Perhaps, this young kid who's now getting everything for free would not understand.

Slowly, everything came alive. The cells were lit up by the sun. We were let open. We had breakfast, but I couldn't finish it. Not because it's unbelievably bland, it was just because my stomach was filled with thoughts and burbs of fear. I tried my best to be as calm as possible and waited for him...

The doors of the big gates opened, I was kicked out of my cell and they were cleaning things up. They moved in a chair, a table, a coat and hung a lantern. I was happy for

This young kid who's now getting everything for free
would not understand.

a moment, seeing my cell getting converted to a luxurious, bright room, but all of my happiness were swept off as I saw the terrible face of the big man. Those same crooked eyes, scars all over his face, the silver Christian cross chain... Mr. Jovial, the big business magnet, one among the JJ brothers.

He gave a faint smile when he saw me, gave a pat on my back and entered the cell which was once, mine.

We were out on the yard the entire time. Luckily for me, we were completely engaged, so I didn't have to enter the cell where the monster lies. But my hopes went to despair, as there was no other option rather than that to enter the cell at night.

As I was walking to my cell, I saw K.K who was kept away from me all day. But we had no time to talk, as I was pushed to my cell by the officer.

And there he was, with a conveniently placed revolver in his table. He was reading a Malayalam book. I entered, had no clue on what would happen and I did not have the courage to go to sleep. The constable duly arrived with a liquor bottle, glass, ice, and mouth-watering chicken fry. I took a deep breath and filled my stomach with that aroma.

I watched him closely as he delicately poured out a glass with ice in it. All these times, he didn't even utter a word. The cell was completely silent. He finished the first glass in a gulp, poured out the second, and immediately turned towards me, pointing the revolver!

I was unmoved... He started speaking, "I have killed many but never have I seen a person stand up for it and take revenge. I'm surprised of what you did in this young age. You are brave and brilliant. I'd love to give you one more chance but you know what, I don't have the attitude of doing so. I just kill them, seeing the same confidence which you have in your eyes turning to droplets of red." He

He delicately poured out a glass.

gave an evil laugh, finished his second glass and continued. "You took a terrible decision, young boy. And I'm afraid that your whole family has to suffer... Bye-bye, young man!"

(thud)

CHAPTER EIGHT

AS IT HAPPENED

(K.K borrows the pen)

That scoundrel of a General posted me for guarding the gates. What kind of a heart does that man have! For a second, I even felt to pull the trigger of my rifle straight to his bald head. I was completely tensed. What about the word which I gave to his mother, who must be eagerly waiting for him. What about my fate? I'm also surely to be killed by him for assisting Kichu in killing John. Oh God! What will my dear wife do?

I stood there, outside the gates. The night appeared to be the darkest one ever. They had already arranged everything. There was an ambulance, doctors, nurses, waiting. My hands shivered. I couldn't help myself. Without me even knowing, my eyes started swelling up, and tears rolled down through my face. My mind was lost in prayer. In fact, I begged to the Lord of the World.

We all eagerly waited for the sound of a shot. Meanwhile, I came up with a decision. If ever at all it happens, I will go there and shoot that man. I don't care of my position or of what consequence I will have to face. I was firm in it. I took my rifle, ensured the bullets, reloaded it and kept it in my hand. I wiped my tears and stood there like a tree, motionless. All throughout my career, I've never been this fierce and confident, perhaps it was my love for an unfortunate kid, a human sympathy, who was more like my own son.

(thud)

And we heard it.... I can't explain what happened. The night became alive. Everyone rushed through. The prison turned into a market, almost. I ran to the cell in the speed of a bullet shot from a gun. I rushed through, and got instantly turned into a statue. My eyes were fixed onto dear, Kichu. His innocent face splattered in blood... That detective eyes were shining, the smile he always possessed didn't fade away. I almost lost my soul but I recaptured it, took my rifle and as firm as ever I took the shot.....!

"K.K, stop! Why the hell are you shooting a dead man!?"

It.....it... it was Kichu who yelled. Everyone stood there amazed. He was alive! By Jove, he was alive! Unbelievable, though it was! The medics, General, other officers gazed at our young Detective in bewilderment!

"How!? I... I thought you were dead... You... You were killed by him."

"Nayy, you think it's that easy to kill Kutti Detective. Hey, you stupid medics, what is over there. Take this guy to the hospital and see if you can do anything and also inject Mr. General with glucose or something, otherwise he will lose his heart." Saying this, Kichu instructed me to open the cell which I had forgot to do and once opened, he left the cell and went to wash his body covered with blood.

The medics went inside, rechecked and took the body of Mr. Jovial which was in a horrible condition. Almost every vein of his, burst out!

The General didn't say anything and he walked over to his office. We all had to wait to get our nerves connected. There was only one person who knew what happened in there and it was Kichu.

He utilised the situation and knew that the officers including the General are now at his command. He instructed them to clean his cell and never to take the things inside brought by Mr. Jovial, out.

After all of that, we were all assembled in the General's office and the news was flashed in the General's TV.

(Actually, Kichu had instructed me to inform the media.)

The headlines were as follows...

"The big business magnet, who owns multiple companies under the brand name of JJ brothers, Mr. Jovial, have suicided. The event happened in the prison and post-mortem is being conducted now. With all the reports we have gotten so far, a young brilliant detective, probably the 'Sherlock Holmes' of our times, called 'Kutti Detective' have extraordinarily exposed his criminal records. He was to be arrested from the prison and maybe even sentenced to death, before this unfortunate incident took place. This incident proves to be a testament to all the criminals who is over-riding people with their influence and money, to be aware! The DGP has taken stance and have promised to take steps to prevent these kinds of things from ever happening again and to bring corruption among his department down! Stay tuned, for further updates. Until then, this is Aishwarya from Indian Times."

CHAPTER NINE

JOB FINISHED

(Kutti Detective continues....)

I walked into the General's office where everyone was present. I was watching the news outside. I could see their awe-struck faces.

"Oh man! That's a lot of praising. Sure to receive a call from the DYSP, soon. Maybe you will receive one too, General sir." I said in a sinister voice.

Everyone's eyes were on me. The General still puzzled, asked to me what happened in the cell, and how is that he died.

"A brave man once said, *To catch a criminal, you have to first think like a criminal.* And that is exactly what I did. Nothing less and certainly nothing more!"

The General threw his glass of water, raised from his seat and shouted, "Speak up, you... I'm sorry.... Kutti Detective...," He remained to his seat and continued, "I'm impressed. It is not that, I don't know to do anything. So, you better don't pull me again or I'm going to put a bullet on your head."

"Calm down Mr. General. Lemme ask you, have you heard of Copper Sulphate (CuSO4)?"

"Yes"

"Hmm, good. In about a second, you will understand."

"Kichu, no you didn't!" K.K sprang into action. "Anyone, call an ambulance quick!"

"What is this! Is it another drama, enough is enough! Damn you, you little... aaaah" The General fell to the floor, gasping for breath. His entire body was starting to bleed and the office was filled with cries of pain. In the hassle of officers running here and there, K.K shouting at me in between, the General took his last breath. The Ambulance arrived, but it was too late. He passed away just like Jovial. The veins which carried the evil-blood have gone. Nothing remains, just happiness and freedom being spread across many.

After the entire round of post-mortem, questioning, court trials, medical checking, the decision was made. Jovial was the culprit. Yes, that's how it went. I don't know how, but it ended like that. That day, I laid in my new cot and took a safe and sound sleep. There was this great satisfaction beaming over my face. Yes, my innocence was proved and there is nothing hindering me other than my dear K.K, who wanted to hear everything, as much as you do. The grand mystery awaits to be uncovered. The story of a perfect execution. The point when I **really** became a murderer.

After continuous nagging, I opened up to K.K. The next day after the court's verdict of Mr. Jovial being responsible, I and K.K was out under the Banyan tree enjoying the sight of the sky and the overwhelming warmth provided by the tree. At one point K.K asked me about it, and I decided it was best that I share it with him.

"You see K.K, I don't feel guilty. No one would. I agree, a crime, is a crime. Even if you rob someone, to help another, it is still a robbery. But in this case, they were already to be judged one day or the other. You itself tell me; how many cases have been registered against him? As you are the 'King of over-sharing', you, yourself have told me about him, and the helplessness of yours and almost the entire department. That is a shame! A big shame! Me, killing him, was not just a statement of revenge but I wanted to protect the world, my nation because I care for it, I care for the people. I might have inherited these thoughts from my father but anyways, Jovial deserved to die, in the most excruciating way possible. Mr. Jovial Jade came here, not to kill me. That was just part of his plan. The JJ brothers were excited about setting up a factory in Maranjarikkad, our wonderful village." I took some time to admire it and then continued, "K.K, that wasn't an ordinary factory, it was going to be the centre for a drug business. I knew all of this, yet not entirely due to my young age. When I shared this to my father, he was alert. He also had suspicions of this happening which was why he ought not to let that happen. That night, we were actually on our way back home after reporting to, well.... That General, who was apparently, a friend of my father. And he back-stabbed us, leading to that traumatic night. About the drug business and all, it was really easy to crack it, my wits and observations helped me do it. My father always took me along with him, so I was able to listen when he interrogated officers concerned with setting up this project. I was present in almost all the conversations, even with the JJ brothers. Though with a limited knowledge, I examined the files, the records and history of John and Jovial which my father had left out.

Their overall nature led me to predict that there was another plan behind this factory. If they set up a drug business, everything is on their favour. Easily accessible routes, raw materials' availability etc....

Naturally, I had deep suspicion that Jovial came here, not for just taking revenge on me because I killed his brother, John. But there was some other intention to it. That's when I found a newly appointed constable who came the same day as Jovial did, Gajan sir, who was more like a servant to Jovial. I was able to interrogate Mr. Gajan in supper time. Basically, a bottle of liquor which I stole from the General's cabin did the work. Absent-mindedly, he shared enough and more.

The papers of that place which they are going to set up a factory is hidden by my father. And absolutely no one has any idea of where it is! They thought that I'd have an answer to that. That was his objective, put me to his gunpoint, and then act like saving me, if I tell him where the papers are. In fact, that was the reason why John came here too. But to their ill-luck, even I don't know about it! Little did they know, I was one step ahead of them. I shot John down and had diluted copper sulphate to Jovial's glass of liquor and at the same time in the water jug of General. I asked Mr. Ali who was himself in a plan of killing Mr. Jovial. He bought me what I needed. You had read to me about $CuSO_4$ and what happens if you consumed it. So, the next thing that happened was, both Jovial and General died in an... well, unbearable way.

Now, you happy K.K. I've told you everything. Now, don't put this topic again or ask me anything about it. Pinkie Promise?"

"Give me a minute. I'm still trying to digest all of that. How did you manage to do all these? I'm surprised, I really am. But I disagree with one factor…"

"What is that, now?"

"If you were able to do all these, you know exactly where those papers are, don't you? Don't worry, I promise, I'm not going to ask anything about it. Let that secret be in your heart. God bless you kid."

I gave an adorable, innocent, beautiful smile. It had been a long time since I smiled like that. All these years, I was bearing a heavy stone. But now it has all crumbled to sand. K.K left me to my thoughts, under the Banyan Tree.

As he was leaving, he reminded me, "One more week to go, Kutti Detective."

Yes, one week…… then, I'm free….

CHAPTER TEN

KUTTI DIARY

1969 Oct 26

A Sunday morning which I will never forget. I could sense the victorious aura around me. It was a great feeling. There isn't much to say about my routine and how it went. You know better than me, what all would I do on a Sunday, don't you K.D? But I can certainly say that the ambience was different. K.K was behind me, almost the entire morning, asking me to narrate what all had happened. It was like a kid asking his parents to buy him this and that. Ah! It was funny. He was my tail today. At last, I told everything under the Banyan Tree. To be honest, I felt better when I spoke out. You should have seen that look on his face when I told the entire story. He was a keen listener and he also pinkie promised me that he would neither talk nor ask about it again. The thing which I'm worried is whether he will share this story of bravery to others. He is the worst at keeping secrets. And I also got a present from Ali. He bought me a cool-looking hat. It was a gift of gratitude for killing Jovial. I took it more like a present and from now on that is going to be my Detective hat. Hurrah!

Then what else, we had our time at the yard, I had cleaning duty and finished my 3 bland courses (of food). I really want to meet the guy who makes food, but I can't complain. We are given ingredients like that. Happy news by the way! This is my 7th year in this place and my last week. Can't wait to see my mother. Good bye for now!

1969 Oct 27

4 days to go! The excitement keeps building up. As for how this day went, it went like all other days. But I feel livelier. I don't know whether it is because I took revenge with the JJ Brothers or is it because I'm going to be released. But it's amazing. Simply great. Today, I spent most of my time in the prison library reading a book which described the meeting of a son and mother. Oh, it was so relatable. I cried in between, imagining me meeting her. How would she be? I'm not getting any more words to say. Fingers crossed.

1969 Oct 28

Today was the laziest day of my life. I spent hours in my cell dreaming. I was in a fantasy world throughout. It was a good day. The new General also came in. A nice fellow. A fat man with a small head, that was how he was. Just before bath, we all had our hair trimmed and looked like disciplined inmates. I was the one who gave the bouquet to the General. He received it with a smile of recognition and laid a soft but kind pat on my back. Apparently, I'm now famous I thought. I wondered what all cases will be approaching me when I'm out of here. Surely, the only thing which I'd miss would be the Banyan Tree. Need to plant one near 'Vishalaya'. Oh, how great would that be! The soothing wind and the overwhelming warmth in one picture. My thoughts were entirely scattered, due to which I got some good beatings, I mean shouting's from the officer. Ya, they are all scared of me now. Some even carries their own water bottle now rather than using the common water point. I'm kind of the hero in the prison as of now. But all of those are to come to an end soon..... Good night K.D.

1969 Oct 29

It was a rainy day today and we had to stay at our cells for most of the time. Other than K.K and the Banyan tree, I didn't have any other friends. Actually, K.K warned me that I should not be friends with anyone. But I couldn't control myself and talk to that person who always caught my eye. He would spend most of his time sitting in the dim corridors looking into the deep blue beautiful sky. He was certainly not the best looking. A good head with a thick hair. His moustache and beard covered most of his face. Everyone seemed to be afraid of him though I've not seen him say or do anything. He was the most idlest person in the 'Junk Crew'. That was the new name of our team. And as the honourable captain of our Junk Crew, I found it best to talk to him. As soon as I received my tea and 'avalose unda', I went straight to him and sat beside him in the corridor. As I gave a glance to the Banyan Tree, I, for real, for the first time K.D, felt like he was talking to me! I felt like it was calling me out to have tea under it and I duly replied, "I have a job to do, companion". My indifferent inmate didn't even seemed to take notice that there was a handsome young man sitting right next to him. I was kinda annoyed at first. But then, I started our conversation by saying, "Salam Bhai" because it suddenly implied to me that he was not a Malayali. Again, he cared less and just said, "Villager" in a soft-sounding voice that too in Malayalam, which I liked. Then, I invited him to the Banyan Tree but he refused due to the fact that the sky cannot be properly seen under it. I already understood that he was not a talkative person but I still suggested the fact that he adores the sky a lot. To which he replied, "not me, my son." Sympathetically when I asked where was he now, he pointed at the sky and said that he was there hiding somewhere behind the clouds. Before I could ask anything else, K.K interrupted me with a firm tone and took me along with him with a few scoldings and reminders. Today, I realised something K.D. Things which we see in our everyday life has a lot more presence and value than we can ever imagine. The Banyan Tree was a little disappointed because his regular visitor was not there in the evening, so he deprived me of the warmth this night. Hope to be friends with that indifferent inmate.....

1969 Oct 30

Today, it was my farewell. Oh, it was wonderful. A party after a long time! It has been a good number of years since I even celebrated my Birthday, precisely saying, 7 years! I might have even forgotten when I was born had it not been for me to step to this world on the same day Kerala was officially formed. 'Kerala Piravi', as it's called. There was ghee rice and some sort of curry which I'm still not being able to interpret. There were shake hands coming from everywhere, officer's **pleasing** looks, K.K really happy, Ali's hugs, and the General's 'laddu'. It was marvellous. The day time was entirely spent on my farewell party. In the evening, everything settled down. As if I immediately turned to a ghost. But I was quite fine with that. All these hears I just have sweet memories with K.K. Other than that, nothing to take away from the so called "school". Of course, I can't forget. I guess I have to give one credit to this prison. For giving birth to 'Kutti Detective'. Otherwise, my life would have probably ended up with me sighing about the past, sobbing and finding some petty job so that I can take care of my mum and myself. For this one and only reason, I say thank you to it. K.D, this diary is completely of my prison life. Quite same, no thrills, no excitement, nothing much to cherish and remember. But things are about to change in less than a day.... Until then, bye K.D.

1969 Oct 31

(I didn't bother to write as I had no time and it was the happiest day of my life. After all formalities, I finally stepped out of a place which had been my world for 7 years. There was surprise and joyfulness in every breath of mine, that I even forgot of my Diary. Hence, this date's account is empty in the K.D.)

CHAPTER ELEVEN

I'M FREE

I packed up my things, took a last glance at my cell and smiled at all my inmates. Astonishingly, I saw our indifferent inmate walking towards me. He came close to me with a pleasing smile on his face and some sort of an envelope in his hands. He laid one of his firm hands on my shoulder and handed me over the envelope and just said, "keep it with you". I gratefully received it and saw him walkaway to his den (the spot he used to sit in the corridor). I didn't have much time to open it, so I stuffed it into my small handbag.

I was wearing a wonderful T-shirt and trouser which my mother gifted me. The General indicated where I had to leave my thumb print in the register and he waved at me saying, "you can safely leave now". I was escorted to the big gates by K.K. The small door flung open as I took a deep breath of the new air and as instructed by K.K, landed my right foot to a new ground. In the midst of enjoying the new and fresh aura, my eyes were wandering for none other than my sweet mother.

I looked right and left but I couldn't see her. Not a lady was there. My eyes started welling up, my body went uneasy, my mind was suddenly filled with haunted thoughts, my heartrate pacing up. I looked questioningly to K.K who was glancing at his watch. Seeing my filled eyes and behaviour, he gave a pat on my back and said, "Don't worry, she's alive."

Hearing those words, my heart came at rest, my mind fully relieved and I wiped the tears from my face. Then, I saw an auto-rickshaw approaching. That surely must be my mom I thought. As the auto stopped, I stared at it with an expectant face. And there a lady stepped out, beautifully dressed, those fine green slippers set foot on the road, there were jewellery in her ankles and wrists, she was wearing some sort of cloth which I didn't know (I later found out that it was called a 'sari'. The only dress I knew were shirts, pants and trousers). But that lady's face was different and her eyes were not fixed on me. Apparently, that was my auntie, K.K's wife. Before my hopes dashed away, I saw another one getting out of the auto. But to my sadness, it wasn't my mother. Rather, it was a small girl almost of my age. Then, an old lady came out with difficulty, her hair was like that of a Zebra's skin; black and white. Her face was wrinkled and there was just a gold necklace on her neck and what was that, oh my god! Those earrings were very familiar to me. Without wasting a second, I dropped everything and gave her, my mother, a big tight hug. Tears of happiness rolled out from our faces and we stood like that for almost 5 minutes till the auto driver started honking. It was surprising to note that she still wore those beautiful earrings which my father gifted to her. His last gift to his dear wife....

We all jumped to the auto and I took no notice of the other passengers (K.K, aunty and the small girl), I was completely busy talking to my mother and I saw her smiling, laughing and enjoying all my stories. Finally, we

I saw an auto-rickshaw approaching.

reached a whole new town which I had never seen. "This is the city", K.K introduced. We reached in front of K.K's house and my mother took me inside to the lavish dining table filled with all kinds of food. It was phenomenal. As we all seated, I finally noticed the young girl.

"K.K, you didn't tell me you had a daughter."

The young girl nodded in disagreement and said that she was my sister, 'Parvathy'. (She was adopted by my mother due to her loneliness and the absence of mine)

I sensed a sudden stop to my mother's heart.

To be frank, I was more than happy to welcome a sister to our life and I expressed the same, to which my mom was relieved. We all, together, had a fine lunch and after that K.K displayed a film on his T.V. From that day onwards, I knew that I, my life, was about to change. I and 'Paru' became best of friends and Aunty, became the best chef. I mean 2nd best, of course. (My mother is always jealous of auntie's cooking)

"That's it my friends, a very brief account of how I reached here, how I became a 'Kutti Detective'. Thank you so much for patiently listening to me. Thank you once again and all the best to all of you!" A thundering round of applause sparked as I concluded my speech and I returned to my chair.

(A briefer version of this was my presentation for the event with a final message of:

> *"Life is unexpected, it may give you disappointments, but it also gives you opportunities in them, all you have to do is to take*

it!)”

49

CHAPTER TWELVE

BONUS CHAPTER

After almost a week spend at K.K's house, I dearly missed Maranjarikkad. So, one day, I asked my mom when we are going to return to our village, to our home. There was a sudden change to her face and she sobbed and said, "I don't think we will ever go back."

"Why not, what's the problem mamma?"

"You see, ever since you and dad left me, I was completely lonely at my place. Until, finally, your Uncle Krishanettan came and suggested me to leave the village and our home and to be settled in the city with them. So, I sold our house. Besides, if we go back there, I don't know what our neighbours will say."

I couldn't stand anymore and rushed to my room closing the door. I jumped onto my bed and started weeping. What all I had imagined to do at Maranjarikkad. I started missing everything, even the Banyan Tree. My mother thought it best not to bother me and left me to my own thoughts. Paru kept on knocking the door, disturbing me and after continuous knocks and calls, I opened the door.

"What happened brother, why did you lock the door?"

"Nothing, simply." It was in her age, I was locked up in a damn cell. An age which was meant to play, ask many questions, and learn about life and the world.

"You alright? Come, let's play. I'm bored"

"Not now, I'm tired. After sometime." She was a sensible girl and understood what I had meant and kindly left my room.

For a minute, I began cursing my life but as my eyes lolled over to my handbag, I remembered about the envelope given by the indifferent inmate. I took the bag, searched for the brown envelope and opened it. Inside, I found 2 photos and a white paper. The photos showed the picture of two old aged men. There were both wearing brown-coloured robes and one had a long white beard up to his chest while the other one was clean-shaved.

"Hmm, monks." I said to myself. "But why has he given me two photos of saints? He considers me as an assassin or something...."

Brooding over my thoughts, I opened the white paper which was some sort of a letter:

Gukesh, is my name. Really glad to meet you. You are the only one who came to me and talked. I am grateful. And so, I feel you can help me. I can't call anyone else, except a kid like you. Sometimes, kids can do better job than us. I trust you.

I was a CBI agent but got trapped and sentenced for life imprisonment. I am from Tamil Nadu, so my English.... Not the best. In the envelope, you see two photos. Monks, one will think. They are criminals. Topmost gold smugglers of India. I want you to catch them, arrest them. Bring them in front of law. I believe in you. In fact, you are the only one whom I can believe. They are in Madras. Please come, meet me and I will share more details.

Trust and beliefs,
Gukesh

My idleness transformed to a centre of energy. A case to crack and out of borders. Thrilling, yes, yes, here the Kutti Detective comes......

(to be continued in...... **'Kutti Detective goes out of Borders')**

Thanks for reading!

- Your fav Kutti Detective :)

Glossary

- Avalose Unda - Rice balls, a traditional sweet of Kerala
- Bewilderment - A feeling of being perplexed and confused
- By Jove - An exclamation indicating surprise or used for emphasis
- Crib - A small bed for a baby or a young child
- Excruciating - Intensely painful
- Hallelujah - God be praised
- Indifferent inmate - Inmate having no particular interest or sympathy; unconcerned
- Kerala Piravi - The birth of Kerala
- Laddu - Sweet from the Indian subcontinent made of various ingredients and sugar syrup or jaggery. It has been described as "perhaps the most universal and ancient of Indian sweets."
- Panchayat - A village council
- Prepping - Preparing something
- Sari - A garment consisting of a length of cotton or silk elaborately draped around the body, traditionally worn by women from South Asia
- Sinister - Giving the impression that something harmful or evil is happening or will happen
- Tuxedo - Black or white blazer worn at formal social events with a bow tie.

Kind Request

Dear reader,

I request you to take a minute and leave a review in the platform you purchased this book. Your words of encouragement or valuable feedback and suggestions means a lot to me.

With gratitude,
Ayham

Reach Out To Me!

Youtube - Kichu Let's English
Instagram - kichu_lets_english
Facebook - Kichu Let's English
Email - ayhambicha2@gmail.com

Coming Soon

KUTTI DETECTIVE

~

GOES OUT OF BORDERS